A Lying Heart

Secret Lies Book II

By Stephanie M. Captain

I0553192

All rights reserved Stephanie M. Captain 2016.

Dedication

To my Lord and Savior Jesus Christ, without you I would
be nothing.

Preface

Sleep escaped me as I knew it would. My body was exhausted and I swore I heard all kinds of noises each time fatigue gripped me in its clutches. For three days I had cried, mourned and hated anything to do with life. Three days I longed for my new found husband. The new husband that had rescued me from the abusive tyrant Finn Bardo. The one that had deceived me into being his maid and punching bag. All I wanted was for Major Jasper to come to me. Rescue me once again. To tell me being arrested for the murder of my late husband was all a mistake. That he loved me and no matter what we would be together. To tell me the evidence that linked him to Finn's murder that I found in our closet that day was all a misunderstanding. To tell me we would be a family as he promised. He had not come. Immediacy was something I craved, but could never find.

Searching the parameters of the outside gate I expected to see my husband when I walked outside of the county jail in the cool March air. Especially chilly in Atlanta for the time of year, I held on to my sweater and my expectation. The only thing that awaited me was sorrow. Sorrow followed me to the taxi that awaited me, sent by the same stranger that posted my bail. A chill ran down my spine that had nothing to do with the freezing weather when I realized I had no place to go, except back.

1

The cold leather glove that was placed over my mouth made me want to gag. Not just from the paralyzing fear that someone was trying to kill me, but the smell of the leather itself made me sick to my stomach. Grimacing in pain I felt felt like my jaw was cracking into pieces. My eyes opened to intense darkness and brutal pain. In the pitch black room I could not even make out a shadow of the figure that pressed hard against my body.

"Don't make a sound!"

The voice was bone chilling. I could hear in it the thrill of an anticipated kill. Like a vampire craved blood he longed to satisfy the killer within. Immediately I made up my mind I would not be his next victim. I had the advantage. I knew my house better than anyone else did in the dark. Terror held me like a cold empty grave, but I refused to die. I would fight for myself. Something I had cease doing long ago. I would fight for the child I carried. I would not abandon my baby in death.

He jerked me from the bed where I had slept for the first time in days. Only because my body and my mind had completely given over to weariness and the fight to stay alert to my surroundings had been lost. He was taking me somewhere and I would not go willingly. Before I ever entered the house where my late husband had been murdered I had a plan. To make it. To fight. Because I knew I had no one else fighting for me. I had made up my mind that even if by some cruel fate I did not survive, it would be a savage battle. I would leave enough discord and DNA so that finding my killer would not be difficult.

"Move!"

When the brazen voice ordered me to move, my insides flinched. I wondered where he was attempting to take me. Why did he not kill me there, where Finn had been murdered? From the feel of the carpet under my feet I was aware that he was taking me through the living room. One, two, three, four, five, six steps; I counted. Reaching out in the darkness, I grabbed the bronze statue that was on the bookshelf in the living room. With a strength that said I am sick and tired of being abused I aimed at where I thought his head might have been.

"Aaaaah!! You ******!!!! I will snap your neck!!!"

Not caring where I had hit him I was grateful it was enough to loosen his grip so I could break free. Memorizing what his voice sounded like for future reference I ran through the house that had truly become my living nightmare. I dropped immediately to my knees after running back through the room because I remembered you never run in a straight line. Maneuvering a low crawl I made my way through the house. The front door was blocked, but there was another way out. A tiny crawl space that lead out through an opening in the garage. Doing my mental count in the stagnant darkness I made my way to the room. Almost there I decided to go in feet first peradventure he found me in the dark. And then I felt him against me. It seemed like my head exploded when once again a hand was placed over my mouth.

Panic set in and with everything in me I used every self-defense technique I had seen on television. Knowing I had hurt him by the jolt of his body I attempted to fight my way to freedom. It was to no avail because he was stronger and more experienced. In the struggle instinct told me that it had not been the same hand that had held me hostage before. There were no gloves. The hand was smaller. The man's physique was not the same. In the madness of my thoughts he spoke to me. Just a faint whisper, "Trust me."

I almost allowed my defenses to weaken when I realized the voice was not the same. As my heart and mind battled, I called to record that I had two strangers, both uninvited, in my house in the middle of the night. The voice spoke again. "I will protect you." I did not have time to respond. There was a crash and I heard footsteps running towards us. The sound of breaking glass made it clear that gun shots were being fired. Jerking me like an old rag doll, this new intruder and I were on the move. Gripping my hand so tightly it hurt, we run from room to room. Then finally through an open window in a guest bedroom we crawled and never stopped running. We run through the green space, past my neighbors and back onto the main road again where there is a car just off the shoulder of the access road. Opening the door he ordered me to, "Lie on the back seat and cover yourself with that blanket."

My body was shaking uncontrollably from shock. Judging by the flow of traffic I guessed it was around three or four in the morning. On the back seat of a strange car, taking me to my death or my deliverance I knew not, I asked God to help me again. Through a peek hole under the blanket I studied his face when light came streaming in from stop lights and traffic. Positioning my head behind the passenger's seat I planned my escape. Making mental notes of street names and billboards I stored the information. After driving for a while I felt the car slow down a bit; then make several turns. Before this stranger would have a chance to harm me I planned to open the back passenger door and run like the flames of hell were trying to engulf me.

When the small car pulled into what I felt like was a residential area I braced myself. With one hand holding the blanket over me I concealed my other hand holding the door handle. I was seconds away from opening the door and running for my life when the car suddenly made a sharp right turn. It sped off back on to the main road, throwing me off the back seat and on to the floor. Fear gripped me again. Disoriented I did not see in which direction we were headed.

"Sorry about that. Are you alright?"

Glaring at the back of the head of my kidnapper I did not give him the satisfaction of an answer. Riding in circles was what it appeared we were doing and I could not connect the dots. At least three times I was certain I could see James Street from my hidden position in the back seat. I wondered why I stayed back there. Was it because I believed he would protect me? Why didn't I scream at the red lights? The only thing I could think of was the distinct differences in the voices I had heard. At least for now I thought being with this stranger was far safer than being with the one that had fired gun shots at us both.

My feet were cold. My shoes had been the only thing I had removed before climbing into the full sized bed in one of the extra bedroom. Completely dressed with a knife under the pillow and a small pocket knife in my bra, I must have drifted off to sleep somewhere in the wee hours of the morning. My hair in a bun to conceal the can of pepper spray from my key chain and wearing loose fitting clothing I had gone to bed calculating my next move. When I felt that hand over my mouth, finding shoes had been the least of my worries.

After about thirty minutes of riding around we turned off the main road again. I could see the sunrise in the distance. The flow of traffic was grossly intensified. Atlanta was waking up and making its Thursday morning commute. My weariness was exaggerated and all I wanted to do was break free. After being locked up for a crime I had not committed I learned something about myself. No longer could I be anyone's prisoner. Clearing my name so I could give birth to the miracle that grew inside of me were the only things on my future agenda. And of course staying alive. Not intending to miss my way of escape I repositioned my arm on the door handle again. When he stopped, for any reason, I was going to make a run for it My chance came sooner than I expected. His phone rang and he fumbled with getting it from his pocket longer than he should have and I opened the door. Prepared to knock on every door in the neighborhood and scream until someone heard me I bolted from that car.

Running through what looked like an older neighborhood in the suburbs, I had no time to think of the dew that felt like ice on my feet. Breaking out and running in a completely foreign place while figuring out which house or yard to take refuge in was not as easy as I projected. Lack of sleep, lack of peace, lack of joy, lack of medical treatment, lack of support and lack of help ran right alongside me. They sprinted through the long distances between the houses on the country road as if we were running partners. Each tag teaming just when I determined I would make it, get through the moment, survive. The footsteps behind me motivated me to keep running more than they could to stop me.

My tunnel vision held the big brick house with the gray shutters on the hill in sight. All I needed to do was reach the door; get within screaming distance. I ran in and out of the tall grass, staying away from the main road. Reaching the black door finally I began to bang violently calling out for help. "Help!! Someone please help me!!!" Running to the side of the house I hit the windows thinking maybe it was just too early in the morning. Making my way to the back of the home I franticly called out while knocking until my knuckles bled. Completing a circle of the home I attempted to return to the main entrance again and tripped. In my tumble to the ground I realized I had tripped over a for sale sign.

All of my hope hit the ground when I did. How could I have missed it? How stupid could I be to seek refuge in an empty home? Wanting to scream, I resolved I could not afford a mental meltdown. Pushing myself up from the ground I decided I had to keep running. With the desperation of a person that did not want to die I got up and once again and I ran. Right into a solid body. The force was such that it knocked me to the ground again. Rolling over in the wet grass I quickly leaped to my feet and came face to face with Major. Terror struck and mentally in a fog I couldn't figure how it could be. I knew his touch, his voice, his body, but my mind said it wasn't possible. He tried to touch me but I stepped just out of his reach. My mind wondered where the man, the stranger, that had taken me from my home could be? Who was the man that had come to kill me? Were they all working for my husband? Was he capable of such an evil? He tried to embrace me, but I shunned him.

"My Love, come to me. I would never hurt you, not ever?"

His voice made me weak and I couldn't think straight. He sounded tired, older. His hair was graying prematurely around the edges of his tresses. He reached out again and caressed my stomach. I couldn't run from him. My legs were weakened from fatigue. My belly felt awkward and heavy for the first time. Evidence of the child growing with me. The child we longed for like a thirsty soul craved water. Once more I tried to put a barrier between us but he was stronger than I was. I didn't want him to touch me. He couldn't touch me. Unlike him, my heart could no longer lie. I loved Major and wanted to believe the best about him; us.

"God I am so sorry love. You are everything to me Taylor and I love you with my whole being."

My eyes questioned his. Why did you leave me in jail? Did you murder my late husband? Why are we in the middle of nowhere with people that want to harm me? Voicing my thoughts were impossible. Hearing reason was effortless. He constantly told me he loved me. Kissing my neck. Holding me tight. My heart could only believe whatever he said to me. My heart still loved him, needed him, and longed for him. I trembled with fear. Shuddered with desire. I was petrified that the man I loved was indeed a total stranger to me. A stranger that meant me harm.

As Major stood there loving me with his eyes and telling me a story that I salivated to hear with his hands, the sound of fire crackers began to fill the air. My reactions just were not fast enough. I watched as a man wearing a mask looked me in the eyes and pointed a gun directly at me from the back seat of a dark colored car as the driver sprayed gravel from the unfinished road. Voices screamed, "Get down!" more shots are fired, more screaming. Tires spinning. I felt my body hit the ground once more with impact that took my very breath away. Someone was on top of me. I could not see, breath, speak, or respond. Then I heard it. Silence. The cool morning air was calm, like a moment with the universe. Still. No sound. Just clouds. Singing. Finally peace.

2

Noise. So much noise. Unwanted and unwelcomed blared in my ears. What had only been a couple of seconds felt like a few lifetimes. Voices were all around me and I recognized none of them. My heart was hurting. My body, my chest, and legs felt so heavy. Forcing my eyes open I saw only darkness. Fuzzy lines. Trying to adjust my vision I blinked and looked again and realized that what was heavy on me was my husband's body. His back, covered in blood, laid on top of me like a steel barge. I whimpered. I stared at the red flashing lights and prayed to the stranger I called God. Time was lost to me. The length of the ride. The calculations of the sirens. My headache was so painful I just wanted to close my eyes and rest in the nothingness.

"Mrs. Jasper…hello there."

Studying the man's face I wanted so desperately to recall if I should recognize him. His name tag read Liam Davis, charge nurse. And then it all came rushing back to me. Frantically scanning the room I saw medical equipment and an empty hospital bed next to mine. When a woman wearing scrubs came rushing through the door I notice there was a police officer standing on the other side of it. Anxiety started to suffocate me.

"You are safe Mrs. Jasper. No one will hurt you now, I promise."

The brown woman, Dr. Anita Keran looked in my face and spoke slowly and kindly to me. I wondered how she could make such a promise. Reaching down I tried to pull out the

IV from my arm. The doctor took my hand in hers and asked if I was in pain. With tears streaming down my face I touched my head with my other hand. She assured me that she could help with that little problem. Then I wondered if the pain medication will harm my unborn child. Ripping my hand from hers I placed them both on my stomach. The terror in my eyes meet the peace in hers and I began to violently weep. All I wanted was for my child to be fine. She reassured me.

"Your unborn child is just fine Mrs. Jasper."

Maybe my face still wasn't convincing or perhaps my eyes mirrored my doubts. Whatever the case she suddenly told me, "I have something for you Mrs. Jasper."

From her scrub jacket she retrieved a small black and white picture and extended it to me with one hand and a box of tissue with the other. Accepting the tissue I dabbed at my eyes wanting to know just what she had given to me. Looking from her to the picture and back again I am unable to really see anything at all. Answering my unspoken questions she leaned in closer and relayed to me, "You are looking at the very first picture of your unborn baby. See, there's the head right there. The legs and feet…" For a moment I felt euphoric and then I thought about my husband. My eyes swelled up with tears again and I had to know what I was so terrified to ask since the moment I remembered.

"My husband…please tell me, I need to know…"

The atmosphere in the room became very solemn. The nurse looked to the physician and the physician grasped for words to say.

"My husband, Miss, please tell me."

I watched Dr. Keran as she pulled up the empty chair and sat by my bedside like she was a beloved family member. My mind did not want to accept that in less than six months I would have become widowed twice. Waiting I held the picture close to my heart.

"Mrs. Jasper, your husband had to be medivacked to Southeast Medical Trauma Hospital where he remains in the intensive care unit. I have to be honest, it doesn't look good, but he has the best physicians in the world giving him medical treatment. The mere fact that he survived is a miracle. My thoughts are to hope for one more."

Swallowing the lump in my throat that I felt would sift the life from me I made a brave show. There was so much I needed to know about the last several hours of my life. Maybe the doctor was the wrong person to ask, but she was warm and easy to speak with. I just wanted some answers; so I asked.

"Why is that police officer at my door?" Someone had tried to kill me. Jumping to conclusions that they were there to help me would have been a ludicrous act. Just like my spending three days in jail for a crime I did not commit. It was all proof that our judicial system was not so just.

"Mrs. Jasper, they are here to speak with you, but only when you feel up to it and I give them medical permission."

"Why wouldn't you give them permission doctor?"

"Because you have suffered a great deal of traumatic events in which you suffered a pretty severe concussion Mrs. Jasper. We need you to stay with us for a couple of days to make sure you are well. Anything they need can wait. For now anyway."

Nodding I struggled to understand the series of events in my life. Events that were bombarding me from every side. Wanting nothing more than to rest my mind I asked if I could be administered the medication for my headache. When the doctor whispered something to the nurse and left the room I closed my eyes again. I had no idea in which hospital I was an inpatient. If my husband would live or die. What would become of me or my unborn baby? Who tried to kill me? Who else wanted me dead? Where my parents were. What condition my home was left in? Whether or not I would have to bury another husband. No answers. No one to call. Just devastation. Like the remnants of the many plane crashes for which I had done litigation I felt piecing my life together again was an impossibility.

My eyes reopened in shock when I heard the nurse's voice tell me that my friend had been waiting for much of the day to see me.

3

When a gentleman walked into my hospital room posing as my friend I did not recognize him at all. Then I met his eyes and remembered everything. A flashback of riding in the back of a car staring at the back of his head and studying his eyes in the rearview mirror assaulted my mind. I immediately reached for the call button. Fumbling because of the IV in my arm and the result of my scarred nerves I dropped the box and it dangled from the bed.

"How are you Taylor Bardo Jasper?"

The way he slowly said my name, my entire name alerted me that something much bigger than I knew was transpiring. Studying his face I registered every detail in my memory bank. He was chocolate. The kind of chocolate that women loved. Low haircut, gentle eyes, and at just under six feet he had an air about him. Testing the waters I answered his question.

"Well. I am well thank you. So kind of you to visit me. My goodness, I just never imagined you would come."

Smiling and revealing perfect white teeth he answers, "Well, why wouldn't Howard Whitt visit such a special person as you are Taylor? After all, it helps having a friend that is also a detective now doesn't it?"

Realizing he was speaking in code I listened intently, and so did the police officers outside my door.

He continued. "Not to mention my old college buddy, your husband would have my legs in a pretzel for not looking after you."

Still not having enough of the puzzle to construct a clear picture I gathered every detail. Approaching my bed he gave me a gift bag and a card. Not knowing what to do I placed the items on my lap. He surprised me when he insisted that I open them right away. Realizing that we are playing a chess game and it is my turn to move I obeyed the quiet stranger. The bag, containing books entitled, Follow The Plan, Trust No Man, and the last one called, Fight Like A Girl were all neatly wrapped baby shower themed paper.

"Thank you so much Howard. I am sure I will enjoy reading all of these in my spare time." The game preceded.

"Not so fast Taylor. You have a card to open now don't you?"

The card, having no envelope, was placed within the largest book, Fight Like A Girl. He stood at the side of my bed, towards the head. A calculated move to conceal my facial expressions. When I opened the card there was a sheet of notebook paper placed within it. I read the note.

'Your husband hired me to protect you. He contacted me while you were still married to your husband, the late Mr. Bardo. He was worried about your return home due to your domestic situation so he paid me $10,000 to be your invisible body guard. I never had the opportunity to fulfill my contract. All I know is that you and your husband are in grave danger Mrs. Jasper. Someone wants you dead and they will stop at nothing until you are. Your husband is in critical condition because he used his body as a shield to protect you and your unborn baby. I had no idea I was being followed. I was sure I did everything in my power to make sure that was not the case. Your husband arranged for me to meet him in an undisclosed place so that he could place you in hiding until we could figure this whole thing out. That is where I was taking you; to meet him. Since the day you were arrested I have worked to get you out but to no avail. He could not see you or post bail for you, which leads me to believe some people in some prestigious positions are somehow involved in this whole mystery. I know you have several questions but they will have to wait until we can speak openly.'

Happy I no longer had a monitor hooked to me to conceal the racing of my heart I did my best not to fall apart publicly. If everything he said was true the only help I had was barely holding on to life in a hospital bed and all I wanted was to see him. The thought of fighting alone scared me. The thought of him being alone battling for his life saddened me.

"Howard, thank you so much." I fought back tears.

"Taylor, I am just happy you liked it."

His eyes were sympathetic. For that I was grateful. As an afterthought he reminded me to finish reading the card. I was puzzled, not about his clue, but as to where to find the remainder of the message. Then I remembered how my mother always went straight to the back of the card looking for the money that was always taped to the back of it by my father. Just as I suspected I found taped to the back of the card under the insert was my husband's credit card. Flipping to the front I found taped there a power of attorney giving me permission to speak as though I was Major Jasper. Taped across the back of the credit card was the word, "Forever." Tears filled my eyes. It was our code word. One that only Major and I knew and had agreed to only use in a life or death situation. That was when I believed everything that Detective Whit had revealed to me in the letter.

When he hugged me he slid the piece of paper from the opened card and crumbled it, then quickly placed it in his jacket pocket. Reaching in the opposite pocket he pulled out a cell phone.

"Oh, I forgot, you left your phone in my car today."

The phone was foreign to me, yet I rejoiced at receiving it like I would have an unexpected Christmas gift.

"Thank you Howard. I was wondering where I dropped it."

"Anytime. Listen, I am going to see my friend tomorrow. Although he is in a coma, the doctors believe that he still hears what is going on around him. Is there anything you want me to tell him?"

There was no need to think about an answer. "Tell him that I love him with all my heart and that he is not getting out of diaper duty."

Chortling a bit, Howard Whitt left the room with a wave; nodding at the police officer as he did.

4

When Dr. Anita Keran sat next to my bedside I was aware that she had shielded me as long as she could. Why she had taken on such a task in the first place was unknown to me, but I was appreciative. The law had been patiently waiting for three and a half days and like a bear coming out of hibernation they were hungry.

"Mrs. Jasper I am pleased with your progress. The way things look there is a grave possibility of you being discharged as soon as tomorrow."

My heart sank thinking about tomorrow. Tomorrow I would be thrown to the wolves. There was no place for me to go. My grandparents were deceased on both my paternal and maternal families. Having moved away as a small child I had no relationship with my other relatives. Being an only child, that left no one. Major and I had not spoken of the secret place for me to retreat should something tragic happen since we had married. For that reason I could not remember just where it was located. We thought Finn had been my only problem, but Finn was gone and my life was still in shambles. Even if I could recall the details, I wasn't sure if I would actually go. His family was as foreign to me as my late husband's, and my own. How could I know just who to trust?

Turning my head away from my physician I wanted to hide the dismay that just kept coming in waves. Dismal, distraught and depressed I was overwhelmed by the state of my life. The husband whom I still loved so much was in a hospital and it did not look as though he would survive.

Heartbroken that he was willing to die for me and I had believed such horrid things about him I wanted to see him just one last time. Learning all the details of his arrest hours after my own helped me understand why he had not come for me. The police were sure we were in cahoots and had planned Finn's murder. They thought by keeping us apart one of us would turn on the other and confess, but there had been nothing to confess. There were still so many unanswered questions that I may not ever know the answers to; especially if I lost my husband. I knew if I was forced to leave the hospital the next day I wouldn't know how to begin putting my life back together.

"Mrs. Jasper I know things are tough for you. Yet, I believe that you and your husband survived such a travesty because maybe a higher power is looking out for you."

Not wanting to be rude because of her kindness I refrained from telling her that what she said was all fantasy. What did she know? Had someone actually been looking out for me I would be at home with my husband discussing baby names. Planning the nursery. Being newlyweds. Instead I had people trying to kill me. The same people that had all but succeeded at taking my husband away from me. The reality that I would never hear what he wanted to say to me that day was eating me from the inside out.

"Mrs. Jasper…Mrs. Jasper…"

"Oh I am so sorry, I guess I must have had something on my mind. Thank you so very much for all you have done for me doctor. You have a wonderful staff of professionals here and for that you should be proud."

When my physician stared down at me longer than she should have I wondered what she actually saw. What was she thinking? I knew there was not a soul in the world that could help me or protect me and my unborn child. Did that reflect in my eyes? My posture? All I could conclude was that life was cruel. Maybe that was what she saw in my eyes. Bitterness of soul, hatred for all people, and a distrust for mankind. Perhaps the world wasn't a place I wanted to birth a child into. She said nothing more.

After she left the room I closed my eyes and hoped that tomorrow would never come. Not the one I must face alone, terrified and mentally exhausted. That night I asked who ever was listening to allow me to die in my sleep. My child and I would be much better off I was certain.

5

Listening to them converse in the other room I felt like I was the one responsible for bringing the Zika virus to America. The wife, very poised, educated and curt tells her husband in no uncertain terms, "Well she cannot stay here."

"But Love, I swear it is just for one night. She has been through much turmoil and just needs to rest until we can figure this thing out."

"Her resting has unequivocally nothing to do with our home. The only thing that matters to me is our little prince sleeping upstairs in his crib."

Her candor was odious at best. Searching for the door to leave I quietly walked through the large home. I could still hear them talking as I went.

"You must obey the rules darling. There are some things you should never bring home and another woman is number one on that list."

The voices were becoming muffled. That was a relief. It meant I was one step closer to finding my way out of the home of the Whitt's. When I stumbled upon the back door I gladly took my escape, only to learn that the gigantic yard was completely fenced in. Feeling like a caged animal I paced the perimeters of the gate repeatedly. Winded from walking in the cool air and not being properly dressed, I took refuge against a tree and thought back to my life just one week earlier.

When the doors of the prison walls had opened, I exited with only the small bag carrying my personal belonging and my unborn baby. The only place I had to go was back to the home my late husband and I had shared. Glad I had gone against Major's advice, I felt a small sense of relief that the mortgage was paid and the utilities remained on. I did not know which frightened me more; returning to the house where my late husband had been murdered or facing the husband that had murdered him. I held that card tightly in my hand that had been dropped through my jail cell as though there was a message in the words, "Go to the secret place." Something in me needed to hope even if everything around me was hopeless. I felt I was framed for a murder of a man who had been nothing short of cruel to me. Abandoned by a man that had sworn he loved me. Handcuffed by men that would not listen to me. The questions would not stop. How could Major deceive me? Murder? The payment of ten thousand dollars. The motives. Was my husband really a murderer?

That was what it looked like to me, but as a lawyer something had not felt right to my gut. Those instincts had proved to be correct. Never would I have guessed that I would be targeted for murder, my husband would be in a hospital comatose, and I would be pregnant and alone at the mercy of strangers.

"You should probably try and get some rest Mrs. Jasper."

The detective's voice startled me so badly I almost stifled a scream. Knowing that people you loved were either being killed or hurt does something to a person.

"Sorry, I didn't mean to startle you. Just got a little worried when I could not find you in the house."

"I was trying to find my way out, but this was the best I could do."

"Oh, did you need to go somewhere?"

Irritated, I looked away. "Detective Whitt, I heard you and your wife and if you would just take me to a hotel I would greatly appreciate it."

"Sorry about that, but you don't have to worry, things are fine now Taylor."

"Right…and my daddy is the Mayor of Atlanta."

"Now that I wouldn't know anything about. However, I do know that you are supposed to be here. My wife understands that I assure you."

"Whatever you say detective."

"In that case, I say why don't you come inside out of the cool air and get some rest. The guest bedroom is waiting for you."

Not having much of a choice I followed him inside. Having just been released after spending almost five days in the hospital I felt exhausted at best. Waiting at the door was Mrs. Whitt. Tall, brown complexion, short sassy haircut colored in the brightest red, she extended her hand to me. After having heard the little discussion between the husband and wife I was reluctant to take it. She sensed my mistrust and decided to leave well enough alone. Not wanting to come off as rude I greeted her.

"Hi Mrs. Whitt. Please forgive my imposition. I promise tomorrow I will be out of your hair. Thank you for your hospitality tonight." I did not look at her. All I wanted was to take refuge in the bed that had been extended to me. My brain hurt thinking of the fact that I had no clothing except the ones that detective Whit had purchased for me to leave the hospital in. A jogging suit, as hideous as it was, not to mention something I would never ever chose. Not even for the cat lady in my parent's old neighborhood. But it was better than the hospital gown.

"Why don't we talk about it in the morning Mrs. Jasper."

Her voice had a forced kindness and a fabricated sympathy; both of which I despised. Nodding my head I acknowledged her proposal having no intentions of being around when Heather Whitt awakened. Walking upstairs the desperation of my circumstances weighed heavy on me. The tears begin to fall the second I closed the bedroom door. Laying fully dressed in the middle of the oversized bed I cried myself to sleep.

6

Sitting on the cold bench at the park, in my estimation, about a mile from Howard Whitt's home I felt utter despair. I was alone. Not just with the swings and the slides, but in a world I had not asked to come into. Even the birds had refused to sing that morning. The grass hid beneath the cold hard ground. The wind in its anger upset the awakening Eastern Redbuds. The white Oaks stood up in defiance to the heavy gusts. Something I knew I could no longer do. My strength was gone.

All I had on me were the credit card and the oversized beach bag that served as my home on the run. Every sound made me paranoid. Loud sounds had the same effect as subtle ones. Each caused me to investigate. Each causing my already anxious heart to stand guard. Memorizing cars and license plates that looked suspicious I longed to just be for a moment in time. To not have to be a permanent residence of flight mode.

It was hard not to ponder the growing life within me. I closed the door when my mind tried to peer into the casket where my late husband had laid. I attempted to cover my ears from the sounds of gunshots that were on a constant recorder. I tried to shut my heart off from the pain that stemmed from not knowing where my parents were. Not knowing if my husband would make it. I longed to see him and deep within me I knew I would stop at nothing until my eyes rested upon Major Jasper. The man I'd hastily married. Did not know enough about, yet loved anyway. The father of my child and the only person that had ever given up everything for me. Watching the small clouds drift, so did my thoughts, to the day of my police interrogation.

An interrogation was exactly what it had been, although Dr. Keran had only agreed to a few questions. When the tall fair Caucasian officer walked into my hospital room, I knew it would be so much more. The Hollywood smile and the rehearsed greeting were lost in his eyes. Green eyes that housed evil behind them. An evil that made me feel certain there was already a special place in hell reserved just for him. Perhaps, for the bodies that might be found in his back yard and basement. Maybe even for unexplained incidents. Incidents that no one bothered to question because he was so perfect. I wasn't deceived, and for that reason I braced myself.

"Mrs. Bardo, or is it Jasper?"

I said nothing. He knew I was aware of what he was implying. The war between our stares commenced for a few seconds. Each of us standing our ground until he relentlessly fired his next round of questions.

"Do you have any idea who would want you dead Mrs. Jasper-Bardo? Is it possible you may have made some enemies during your prison stay? Or maybe the family of your late husband may still be upset about the unexpected, untimely death of their beloved son, brother, and grandson. By the way how is your husband these days Mrs. Jasper?"

The question sent an electric shock through my being. I had no idea what the status on my husband's current state could be. Somehow I was certain he knew this. Anger began to swell inside me. Anger that he had not missed and slavered after it. As I stared at him my instinct told me that Officer Monroe wanted me to give him a reason to add me to his list of victims. Approaching me and coming too close to my personal space he demanded, "Answer the question Mrs. Jasper." Rising to the occasion I was prepared to match his defiant attitude with my own. Exhausted from the uncertainties of my life I was prepared to stand up for myself, even if it meant going back to jail. The tension in the hospital room was that of a cold war.

"You killed your husband didn't you? Then you tried to cover it up by having your current husband executed. It was clever how you made it look as though you were the target. Why? Why did you do it Mrs. Jasper?"

When he yelled so loudly again for me to, "Answer the %#** questions!" I flinched inside. Sitting up in my chair so he could see the rage in my eyes I decided to defend myself from the asinine, bigot that stood in front of me.

"You..."

"Mrs. Jasper you need your rest. We must keep you and that precious little one in good health. I am certain that your husband has two good reasons to get well and we shall not disappoint him shall we?"

My blind rage had prevented me from seeing Dr. Keran reenter my room. Her comment was like a slap in the face to the arrogant, pompous defender of the law. Looking from her to me I made sure I held his eye as I said, "Doctor, I believe you are correct."

Unwilling to release the reins of injustice he protested. "I still have a few more questions."

Dr. Keran's professional, but firm dismissal was one he could not deny. "Understood Officer Monroe, but your questions may not interfere with my patient's care. Right now the best thing for her is rest. Perhaps your department can make other arrangements once she is discharged. Or maybe you could arrange a meeting with Mrs. Jasper's attorney. For now, she needs rest, doctor's orders." Holding the door open for him to exit, the exasperated and defeated officer had no other recourse but to walk through it. Thinking back, that day is on the top twenty list of my worse days.

Letting out a sigh I continued to watch the drifting clouds as my mind eased back into my current reality, until my peripheral vision picked up a reflection. Nothing huge, but the slightest hint of a shadow that was cast upon the end of a shrub. Just enough to alert me that I was not alone. Already high on adrenaline, I was careful not to make any sudden moves until I knew which way of escape I should take.

Behind me was a trail that lead to a wooded area. Instinct told me that was the area to avoid at all cost. My only other option was either to try and out run whomever was after me or run directly into the busy highway. The chances of me making it back to the Whitt's home were against me. Who could out run a bullet? Yet, the steady traffic of the morning commute could be just as deadly. Before I could decide a masked man came from the direction of the main entrance. I grabbed my bag intending to use it as a shield or a weapon and threw myself onto the street. Hearing the screeching tires and blaring horns that followed were a consolation because it meant my baby and I were still alive.

Panic seized me and I stood paralyzed in the middle of the street. Two masked men starred down from the top of the small hill in which I had just jumped causing traffic to come to an abrupt halt. None of the obscenities being spewed at me helped my feet to become unglued from the pavement. In that surreal moment I lost all hope. My brain could not comprehend what to do next. Should I allow fate to carry me off to its will or should I pick my poison and die at my own hands and just lay down in the oncoming traffic? Either way, it seemed death was imminent. Running from it was no longer possible.

Looking up to the sky I wanted to scream at God. Why! Why! Some people say you are not real. Yet others give their lives because they are certain that you are. You never gave me a chance to know either way. What do you want from me anyway? Why was I even born? You are the only one that knows who I am and where I came from yet you are silent! How can you expect me to give so much and you will not give me the help you know I need! You want me to believe in you, then prove that you are who others say you are? Why am I going through this? What about my husband? My child? What happened to Finn? My parents? Who killed Major? My heart was desperate. Stripped of any hope. Hemmed in between people that would stop at nothing to kill me and traffic that was unmerciful I looked up from my downward stare and directly into the eyes of a stranger.

Sure I was having an out of body experience I could only stare into my eyes. At my own mouth. My nose. My lips. My tortured mind did not comprehend that the skin color and the hair were slightly different. All I knew was that I saw myself, yet it wasn't me, and went into shock.

"Get in! Now!"

I obeyed her. Why I did is a mystery. It could have been the fact that I had nowhere else to go. Maybe something down inside told me it was a safe move to make. Or it could have been the apparent shock. All I know is that I jumped into the open door of a car with a woman I had never met, but was positive I already knew.

7

"Put your head down! Now!"

Slamming the door closed I followed orders as we sped away. Despair ridden I followed instructions once again when she ordered me to "Put on my seatbelt, and hold on!" I had nowhere else to run.

Unbeknownst to me, I had been spotted by not only the assassins, but this third stranger I now rode with. I wondered if she viewed me as the crazy woman who had jumped in the middle of a busy street. Standing completely paralyzed in the middle of the road way clutching her bag. Now, sitting next to her I was at a loss for words. Her command had been impulsive. I later learned the search for me had been long and she had never actually rehearsed what she would say when finally she met her face to face. I could tell she was grasping for the right words to say as I watched the woman from my peripheral vision. Before she could find them I set the record straight.

"Look lady, I don't know who you are but if you are going to kill me just go ahead. I'm tired of running anyway. I don't have anything to give you so you are just wasting your time. So just do what you are going to do."

Not being able to look in her direction for fear of being followed she drove as fast as she could in an effort to alert the police. I assumed that they were busy that day. After riding around for a while she eased onto the freeway and headed to the airport. She said nothing until we pulled into the car rental parking lane. Little did I know that my life was about to take another major turn when I allowed her to tell her story.

~

"Come on, we have to move quickly."

Surprisingly Taylor followed without protesting or trying to make a run for it she continued to walk with urgency. I saw so much of myself in her in my early days of running from despair, depression, and death. The days after my own mother's death. The woman that had been the only mother I had known until she had been killed in a car crash when I was twelve. Then life as I had known it ended. That was when I began to live a prison sentence with my custodial guardian. A life that was filled with pain, despair and hatred.

Having already made reservations for the new rental car the stranger insisted she must have local license plates. Luckily, the process was remarkably fast. After making sure we were not being followed I redirected Taylor into the restroom at the airport. Once inside I hold up a note to her. "Say nothing at all." She nodded her head. The fear instantly returned. I notice her immediate tension.

Cringing within I ponder just how little I know about Taylor Bardo Finn's life and silently prayed to God for help. Pulling out another note from her bag she explains her actions.

"You may have some type of tracking device on you."

Looking at her face I observed her expressions go through just about every emotion and then finally reason showed up. That was when I extended my final note.

"Strip down. Leave everything. Even your bag and phone."

When I gave her the tote I had been carrying, Taylor took it and went into the handicapped stall.

When Taylor walked out of the stall she wore the palazzo pants and loose fitting shirt from the bag. She tried to keep her old shoes but that would have been another ideal place to keep a tracking device. Especially with her only having a limited wardrobe. I sympathized that she would have to wear shower shoes in the cold, but it had been my only recourse. Having to guess Taylor's clothing size had been easier than figuring out shoe sizes.

When I removed the hair piece that held Taylor's pretty reddish brown hair in a bun and threw it in the trash I could tell she was irritated. I reached into my purse and took out the ponytail holders and hairbrush and gave her a nice ponytail and a trendy little hat. I could tell Taylor liked it. I smiled. It was my way of apologizing. It wasn't until we pulled into the valet parking of a five star hotel did I notice Taylor's jaw line relaxed a bit. I was certain she was frightened, hungry, mentally and physically exhausted. She recognized every emotion Taylor's body bore. Despair had also been my cloak for far too many years.

Once inside the secured room on the floor that only those with key access and a code from the front desk could enter, Taylor did something that I herself had done for all of my teenage years. She crawled into the middle of the bed into a fetal position. Seeing it broke me inside. For just a moment in time I was back in my custodial guardian's home.

When that space of time passed I had no doubt God had purposely allowed me to feel those emotions again. It was the only thing that made me stick it out with her. Cassie, or Taylor, as she had been renamed; was in far more trouble than anyone knew.

I walked over to her and sat next to her on the bed. Taylor does not move. I rubbed her back like the mother that had abandoned both of us should have. Like the other parents that both of us had been given were supposed to. The only song I knew that made her feel better was the one I had sung to myself. The one my adoptive mother had sung to me until the day she died. The one my mother still sang to me in my dreams. The song that I sung to a God I did not know at the time and was not sure He even existed.

"Yes, Jesus loves me. Yes, Jesus loves me. Yes, Jesus loves me, for the Bible tells me so."

Just when I believed Taylor was fast asleep, she jumped to the floor and demanded to know, "Who the **** are you?"

Not wanting to add to the already stressful situation I extended my hand.

"Hello, my name is Hannah and you are my sister."

It had taken less than an hour to explain that she was the sister that our mother had given up at birth. The same mother that had hidden the fact that she had given birth to a second child and hid her until she was around three months old, but had not been able to keep her. This same mother that was now ill and the guilt of what she had done to her little girls tormented her daily. The story, far-fetched, complicated, and disturbing could be proven by a simple DNA test.

After hearing Hannah out, Taylor Jasper remained in bed for two days. Only eating, sleeping, and bathing when her big sister Hannah Renee Corel-Waiters Emmanuel forced her to do so.

8

It had been one month since I was bailed out of jail. A month of hell with sleepless nights and days where I wished the sun had never come up. One month since my brief moment with Major, before he had been gunned down right before my very eyes. Before he had shielded me with his body, saving my life and our unborn child's life.

Pushing the cart into the hospital room I felt like a fugitive. Not from the law, but from those desiring to kill me. It was not rocket science knowing that my husband's hospital room would be the first place those seeking my life would look to find me. Determined to stop at nothing I wasted no time calling my late husband's grandfather for help. Money talked and the Bardo's had plenty of it. It was easy convincing him that I wanted nothing, only a favor. A huge favor. Although I felt as though promising to give him one afternoon of my time to settle matters was like walking into fire douched with gasoline. I agreed anyway. He kept his word, as I knew he would and got me into the hospital through the janitorial system.

Entering the room quietly I had to stifle a gasp when I saw my husband. The pain was so deep within me that the baby took refuge right next to my bladder; adding to my pain. He did not look like my husband. His face was swollen, his skin pale and blotchy. The blinking machines, the tubes, the stillness were overwhelming. Feeling lightheaded I held onto my cart and took deep breaths. My recovery had to be swift because I knew his room was being monitored by the nurse's station and the people looking for me. For that reason alone it had to be convincing that I was the replacement of Maxine O'Riley. A hospital staff member that just happened to be sick that day.

My taking refuge in the restroom would not appear strange. After all, it was a logical move. Bathrooms being a part of my cleaning duties, it was lucidity. Turning on the facet at full force I took asylum in the toilet. Vomiting up all of my anxieties and fears took longer than I was comfortable with. My heart was pounding and my hands shook so badly I dropped my cleaning solution twice as I pleaded for help from the God Hannah knew so much about. Hoping that I had not startled Major or alerted anyone else I became even more frantic. Longing to go to my husband and reassure him that I was there for him made my very heart bleed. Needing to tell him that I still loved him with all of my heart and that our baby was fine got the best of me.

I went through the ritual of cleaning the restroom like an actual employee was expected to do; all the while knowing that I would risk it all just to touch my husband. To tell him that we were still on the same team. It was hard to determine if the eyes that stared off into nothing would actually see me. Or if the brain that was declared not as active as they like to see would hear or comprehend that I was even there. I wanted to think that the bond we shared would penetrate the heart that slowly beat. If I could just whisper in his ear.

The closer I got to the hospital bed the more I realized how much I missed and loved my husband. There were so many unanswered questions, but I still knew the only reason he was in the intensive care unit of Southeast Medical Trauma Hospital was because he loved me. Emptying the waste receptacles, then sweeping the floor, I tried to hold on to his last words to me. 'God I am so sorry love. You are my everything Taylor and I love you with my whole being.' They played over and over in my mind ever since that awful nightmare had become my reality.

I was beginning to believe in God more. It had begun the day I stood in the middle of the street in utter despair screaming up into the heavens from the depths of my soul. The day I faced two assassins at the top of a hill and the truth that I had nowhere to run. Nowhere to hide. Then from the air appears a total stranger. Stopped in front of me demanding I get in her car. The day I heard the words, 'Hi, I am Hannah and you are my sister' I could no longer deny His existence.

When I leaned over in pretense to dust the bottom bed rails I seized the opportunity to whisper a message to my husband. My back to the door, not wanting to take a chance on anyone reading my lips, I spoke one word to him, "Toujours." It was painful remembering the countless times he had whispered the word in my ear during our love making. When we couldn't agree on something. When he had seen the pain of my past resurface in my eyes made me become careless. Just needing to touch him I grabbed his hand and squeezed it. Repeating the word again a little louder. "Toujours."

When the alarms begin to sound fear seized me. The room immediately filled with white coats and scrubs. Standing in the distance I did not know what was happening or what I should be doing. Nothing came to mind except maybe the

God Hannah spoke of so fondly had brought me to my husband's bedside to be with him in his death.

"Ms. You are going to have to finish that at another time."

The arm pushed me towards the exit felt like I was being sent to the abyss. Trying to conceal the tears rolling down my face I whispered, the English version of our secret word in to the atmosphere. "Forever. Forever my love".

Walking down the long cold hallway I hurriedly sought refuge not realizing I did not have my custodial cart with me. Swatting at the tears I turned back with urgency knowing without it my disguise could be blown. Reaching the room in record time I stopped short hearing someone say, "He is breathing over his ventilator." Then another said, "What in the world is going on? Out of all the days in the world he chose today to wake up." That is when I realized I had been holding my breath.

I had not seen the nurse until she was standing over me staring at my name tag. "Excuse me Ms. Parks but you are going to have to service this room later.

Speaking up rather quickly I said, "Understood. I just need to grab my cart and I will be out of your way." It only took a few seconds to gather my things, but I could not leave without seeing him one more time. Looking over towards the bed, my legs grew weak when our eyes met. He saw me. Had heard my voice and turned in my direction. Needing to run to him and reassure him I froze once more. Until the nurse said in an aggravated voice, "Ms. Parks" you must leave. Now." That is when rather loudly, so

Major could hear me clear I repeated, "Toujours." Looking back one last time before clearing the door he was still staring at me.

9

"Come home Love." His voice was laced with emotion. One of them Hannah recognized as passion. The others she was unable to identify because of the plethora of emotions she was warring through herself.

In her mind she was imagining his perfect physic, his creamy skin, and the gorgeous eyes she loved so much. All of her wanted to run home to him. Except the tiny little hole in her heart that time had not managed to heal. The hole that was destitute without knowing who she really was. That part was the sole reason for her reply to the husband she loved and adored.

"She's my sister Gabe. She is in trouble and for once I want to be there for someone like you are for me. Can you understand that?"

"But it sounds dangerous. If something were to happen to you I…" His voice trailed off. On the other end a tear rushed down her cheek. She was relieved they were not on a video call. The thought was unbearable for her too. The Engineer and the Physician had something that few did. Something that time or trouble had not been able to destroy. Needing to change the subject she asked, "How is our little tribe doing?"

That made them both smile. Their family meant everything to them. Still imagining the 6'4" dark haired, strong chin, and luscious lips catholic boy who had all but swept her off her feet she shifted her mind to what her husband and best friend was telling her.

"Can you believe that I triggered the smoke detector? By the time I got the situation under control Joy had Chance in her toy stroller headed to our emergency meeting place?"

"Yes. I actually can." Her laugh was one of pride and dismay.

"She'd put one of her coats on him and they were both in the back door by the time I caught up with them. Chance gave me the save me daddy she is at it again look. It took all I had not to laugh hysterically."

Her heart melted hearing him speak of their children. The children he loved unconditionally although neither of them looked anything like him. The fact that he referred to their son as Chance, rather than his pet name, BJ did not trouble her. Not being able to acknowledge that he was Brice junior was not his reason for being the only one that used their almost two year old's formal name. Dr. Gabriel Emmanuel called his son Chance because it reminded him of what God had given to him in his wife and children. According to him, he was the luckiest man alive.

"So what in the world did you burn this time Gabe?" Her tone was teasing.

"Well, see, uh I was trying out this new recipe."

"And why? You are sexy. Exciting. Great at everything you do, except cooking." She laughed again. "Why do you think I prepared two weeks of dinners before I left?"

"So it's like that? I am uncertain if I should be flattered or offended."

"Flattered. Definitely flattered. One out of a thousand isn't bad at all."

When the words spilled out she knew they had been a mistake.

"Come home my love." The deep desire his voice was laced with made her heart palpitate with emotions. She missed them immensely. Never had she left her family behind. Not the two children she would take a bullet for nor the man that she had sacrificed the only family she had ever to be with. Those thoughts alone could make her hail a taxi and get the first flight out. But then there was Cassie, or Taylor Jasper, as she was known. The sister she never knew existed until her dying birth mother had been too troubled to go peacefully into the night. The one that she wasted no time having DNA test to prove that their genealogy were one in the same. The sister that was recently widow, remarried, jailed, on the run, and very much pregnant.

"Not fair Gabe. So not fair. You know I cannot handle that voice. Please give me another week and I assure you I will be taking great care of the good doctor."

Groaning inside he gave her the permission she needed. They made small talk for several more minutes until daddy duties called away the man with whom God had given her a second chance at love.

"I love you forever ever Gabe."

"You are the only one for me Hannah. Come home soon please because we miss you. Talk to you soon Love."

46

As an afterthought he had to know, "What about Tobias? Has he responded to any of your phone calls?"

They both knew the answer to the question but still it was asked way too often. She sighed.

"No Gabe. Nothing yet." It was always her answer. She refused to believe that he would never forgive her. That he could possibly be angry forever. Or could he? Distaining her thought pattern her mind shifted back to the matters at hand. She had one week.

10

Exactly twenty-four hours after I visited the Intensive Care
Unit of the city hospital disguised as staff, Detective Whitt
and Hannah Emmanuel walked into a different room.
Having been moved to a less critical area of intensive care
it was a much different scene than hours earlier. Howard
Whitt was hopeful when he saw the look of recognition in
Major's eyes when he greeted him.

"Friend, it is awesome to see you again."

Major Jasper gave a brief wave. His memories were still
returning slowly. Bits and details one dream like state at a
time. Connecting the dots was getting easier, but with that
ease became a constant heartache. Heartache that made him
watch the door continuously. Hope. Long. Regret. He
looked to Howard for answers to problems that had been
unsolvable.

"Major, this is my friend, Hannah." Howard thought it
better not to confuse the situation by revealing Hannah
Emmanuel's true identity. For his sake and her safety. The
less she knew the better. Hannah had a much different take
on the matter.

Walking straight to his beside Hannah grabbed his hand
and gave him a firm squeeze. One that told a story in itself.
"So glad to finally meet you. I have heard so many
wonderful things about you Major."

Not knowing if she was yet another memory trapped in his
past that had not found its way to the future yet Major gave
a half smile. He wanted to speak, but it had proven to be a

very painful experience and he decided to just rest. At least until the right moment came along.

Understanding that the men would have much to discuss Hannah sat in the chair taking in the details of the room. Four beds. A nurse, stationed in the room at all times, while another came and went constantly and watched the monitors and administered medications. The only privacy was that of a multicolored curtain. It was used only when the patients were being examined or the doctors were consulting with family members. Even then the conversations could still be heard. The truth was none of them cared. They were all still very ill. Some had been there for weeks and others for days. Either way they wanted the same thing, just to go home with their families and live again.

Needing to do something Hannah snapped a picture and sent it to her sister. She immediate replied. "Tell him I love him please." Thinking better of delivering such an intimate message Hannah got up from her chair and walked to the bed once more. By the time she got there she could hear a distant "Hello." She put the phone to the ear of Major Jasper.

Wondering if there was a bad reception Taylor continues to say, "Hello…hello…"

Major recognized his moment had come sooner than he expected. Grabbing ahold to the bedrail he managed to force out, "Toujours."

When Taylor heard his voice on the other end of the phone she wept. Through the sobbing she answered, "Forever." Nothing else needed to be said for the moment. He closed his eyes and rest his head on the pillow. Several miles away Taylor sat in the middle of the floor in a hotel room clutching the pillow from the bed. Although husband and wife were miles apart, in that moment they were together and that was all that mattered.

Hannah was all too familiar with the presence in the room. The struggle of love, loss, war, tragedy, heartache, sickness, and pain. She knew it all too well. Had lived it, breathed it, slept with it, and even married it. Only to have to bury it and start all over again. Seeing the struggle of a strong man who could not do what he longed to do, be where his soul already resided, was like watching a victim drown knowing there was nothing you could do to save them. Seeing that anguish caused her mind to wonder back to the day she had first met Taylor Jasper. The reminiscing did not last long before it was interrupted by Detective Whitt.

"Hannah, here is your phone." I was so deep in thought I had not heard Detective Whitt approach me. For that I kicked myself a thousand times. For no reason could I allow my guard or defenses to be down. Someone was trying to kill my newly found sister. They had succeeded at murdering her first husband. They had almost been successful at murdering her had it not been for her current husband using his body as a shield to protect her. My association with her made me a target as well. All I wanted to do was force her to come and live with me. At least until the baby was born, but I was sure she would refuse. She would never leave the man she loved. That was something we both had in common.

11

I sat on the floor of the hotel crying once again. This time they were bittersweet tears. Major had spoken to me. Just one word. An oath between the two that no other human was privy to. My husband was getting better. It was the best news I had received in weeks. I wanted to scream it from the rooftop. Run to his bedside. Touch him, see him, but I knew she could not. Not if I ever wanted to see him again. Or better yet if I wanted to live to see him again. It was clearer than ever that I was the target. Someone wanted me dead and was going through great lengths to carry out their desire.

My brief moment of solace slipped away all too quickly. Chased away by the thoughts of a grave reality. Someone had a contract out on my life. My parents, or the people who had raised me, were still missing. Perhaps dead. I was now very much pregnant and alone. The only people I had helping me were Detective Whitt and Hannah. Hannah, a sister that I never knew existed. A past I could not believe I had. Adopted. Birth mother. Father unknown. None of it made sense to me. So many pieces of a puzzle and none of them fit. Nothing was rational. The only real thing I had was my love for my husband and the baby the kicked and squirmed inside me.

By the time Hannah and Howard returned to the hotel room I had a new fight within her. Hearing my husband's voice had given me hope. It had reminded me of who I was and victim played no role in my saga. I was a fighter. A lawyer. And a darn good one at that. I was trained to see what no one else saw. Go beyond the perimeters that others were allowed. I had concluded that my half-sister had been correct in suspecting that I may have been wearing a tracking device of some sort. It was the only logical thing. The other thing I concluded was that somehow I was a threat to someone. I had something of value and whomever it belonged to would stop at nothing to have it back. Who these people were and what they were was the mystery that had to be solved so I could get on with my life.

Sitting on the floor I used the notebook paper from the hotel desk to piece together a thinking board and did not stop brain storming until the room door opened. Hannah, seeing that look, one we both possessed, sat right beside me ready to join the battle.

"So what do you have Cassie, I mean Taylor?" Looking apologetically at me Hannah almost grimaced.

Jokingly I tried to ease the tension. "Oh it's okay, I kind of like the name. I always knew I did not look like a Taylor anyway."

Detective Whitt observed the interaction between the two women. They could almost pass for twins. He was a good judge of character and people. His job demanded it. Although still awkward at times, they were already forming a bond. Anyone looking on knew they were related. Their accents were very different, but their mannerism were one in the same. Both fighters. One sassy and defiant, the other quiet and observant. Both could be dainty and dangerous to anyone that stood in the way of the people they loved. Taylor, compliant, but calculating. Slightly taller than her older sister was a bit too trusting until she had had enough.

The other, Hannah, went straight to the jugular and asked questions later. You would never know she was coming until it was too late. A classic case of brains and brawns distributed in both ladies made him know that he had better stick close. Plus, get some back up because he was sure this thing was bigger than any of them knew. Having no way to prove his theory he believed the instinct that had never lied to him.

"Hey are you going to earn your keep or continue to be mesmerized by all this beauty? Don't let me tell your wife. I already know she might be a little over protective of such goodies."

The laugh that roared from Howard Whitt did not fit his frame. Taylor looked at the two wondering if her newly found sister was flirting or jousting. Before she decided Hannah had already moved on to something else.

"So what do you have here?" It was all that was needed to compel my investigative and intellectual skills to go to work.

"Well from the time line of things I have figured out that I am the only common denominator. Although my late husband was murdered, who he was and where he was involved me. The recent disappearance of my parents. The fact that the day Finn was killed on the original date I was supposed to return home. What I don't know is why."

The detective in Howard Whitt stepped forward. "Do you know of anyone that would want to take your life? Do you have any enemies?"

A bit annoyed, I snapped back, "Up until all this transpired I thought I was the most boring, miserable person in the world. Now I find out even that isn't true. Turns out I have no clue who I really am."

Getting a revelation Hannah interjected, "Someone knows. Maybe that is the answer."

I don't know, but I do know that my answers are in my house. The one I shared with my first husband. I am certain of it. I have to go back."

Immediately Detective Whitt and Hannah began to protest. It was too dangerous. Too soon. Too much had already taken place in the house. I heard none of it. My eyes were glued to the local news and that had somehow gotten my attention...

"The community of Jonesboro is shaken tonight as two bodies were found in an area lake. The bodies, discovered by contestants in an annual fishing tournament, have yet to be identified. Local police are asking if you have any information concerning this sad situation to please call in.

"It is indeed a sad situation."

"Hopefully someone knows something about this tragic mystery and these poor souls can be laid to rest."

"Indeed. Coming up your weekend forecast. Stay tuned.

For and instant I felt like I had lost my mind. I could not think. Feel. It felt like a light that had always burned had suddenly gone out and I was grouping around in the darkness trying to figure out where I was and what I should be doing. Who was I? Where was I? What should I be doing? Why did my head hurt? My chest?

Hannah saw it first. The look. One she had gotten a glimpse of all too many times in her own life. It was like one could not explain it. Describe it or even control it. Unless you had been there, you would never know what there looked, felt, and sounded like.

"Taylor…Taylor honey what's wrong?"

When Howard looked up from the thinking board, for the first time in five years he actually wanted a drink. The case that had just fallen into his lap he knew of a certainty had just gone from bad to worse. He had no idea though how horrific things had become.

12

Several hours later our three weary souls sat in a dreary room. Voices were hushed. Eyes shifted from one person to the other. Strangers came and went. The old gray door continuously opened and closed. I sat weeping. Hannah held my hand. Detective Whitt asked questions, and many of them. No one had answers. All the police department knew was that the case was becoming larger than they imagined, and the dots were not connecting.

"Mrs. Jasper, please accept our condolences from the police department. I assure you we are doing everything within our power to find out what happened to your parents."

I wanted to tell the short, stocky, young man that resembled one of the chipmunks that I really did not comprehend anything that he said. But just opening my mouth would exasperated me. I felt like I was in a nightmare. One that my entire body reacted to, and my mind was unable to separate from the dream state and reality state. Only it wasn't a dream. It was my life and the only strength I had was used to just breathe.

Hannah squeezed my hand. For some reason I could not explain, it gave me life. Each time my sister drew close I felt a warm sensation flow through my body and my thoughts became clearer. My weaken legs, my aching heart, and my feeble mind that told me to give up felt a release from its numbing grip.

Lieutenant Afton continued to speak in an authoritative, yet monotone voice. "Your safety is important to us so, until this investigation is over, we are placing you into protective custody. Both of your houses are under heavy surveillance as well as the hospital room of your husband."

Hannah breathed a sigh of relief and whispered a thank you that was audible to all in the room. No one questioned her behavior or to whom her gratitude had been displayed.

"Let me introduce to you Officer Tale Carmen, Officer Hunter Bates, Officer Bain Green, and Officer Cynthia Faison. Become well aquatinted with them, because until we find some answers they will be your shadow. When you move they move. Do not, from this moment on go on spontaneous walks, unplanned trips, or even to check the weather without them knowing. Everything you see, hear, find or even remember is important."

When the tears started again Hannah immediately gave me some tissue. Rubbing my back, she silently prayed for help. Having been through much heartache she not only empathized with her long lost sister, but she grieved with her. She understood pain that no medication could alleviate, sorrow that no words could erase, and waves of despair that swept through your life like a category five storm.

The torment that sorrow carried was too much and I leaned in on my big sister of only about ten months. Having had so many tragedies in such a short period in my life I could only live in moments. Not days, hours, or weeks, not even minutes, but moments. Just to breathe. To walk. To talk. To wish things were different. For a long time I hid being physically abused by my late husband. Major had been the first person I had ever opened up to. I had a natural distrust for people, but Major had given me something I had lacked for so long. The heart that I had trained and forced to be loyal had betrayed me. He became my friend. Then my confidante. My counselor. My husband. Then my enemy. Then again the one I could not live without. If only he could just hold me. Tell me what to do. Help me. Kiss me. Reassure me that it would all be fine.

"Mrs. Jasper, are you well?" The concern in the Lieutenant's voice mirrored in the eyes of all in the room, but especially Detective Whitt's. His heart was heavy for the woman that seemed to have had it all just a few short weeks earlier. The career, the house, the perfect husband, and then everything had gone wrong. The kind of wrong that most did not recover from; he wondered if she would. He wondered about the baby she carried. The husband that was still an inpatient in a progressive care unit. The family of her ex-husband, the one that had been murdered in their very home and she was wrongfully jailed for it. His mind pondered the incredible pain her heart must be holding at learning that the two bodies pulled from the river had been her parents. The life of Taylor Bardo Jasper had disintegrated and details of it were still a mystery.

"Are you alright Mrs. Jasper." The question is repeated.

When I did not answer my newly found half-sister took control of the situation.

Hannah stood up and spoke with such authority that none questioned. None. "She has had enough for one day. Due to the severity of the situation, and her current vulnerable state, (all knew she referred to the pregnancy), she will not be residing in either one of her properties. My husband and I have leased a rental property not far from the police department and this is where my sister will be residing until all of this can be resolved. Now, as soon as you are ready, we would like to leave so she can get some rest. I am sure you understand."

When we finally pulled into my new Victorian style duplex it was sunset. The quiet street, just a couple of blocks from the police department substation was ideal. There were only about eight places of residency. No stranger could become lost in the serene apartment scenery and an intruder would surly stand out. The streets were well lite and there were surveillance cameras throughout the gated community.

Although Hannah knew I was mentally and physically exhausted, she would not allow me to be ignorant to my surroundings. So with reluctance as soon as we entered the apartment she gave a tour of the home and covered every possible route to the home, and every way of escape.

The home was stock piled as to not allow me to be seen in public. When and if I needed to leave the apartment it would be with the two officers and it would only be to have maternal care for my unborn child or visit my husband. Even then, it would never be the same time of day, nor in the same vehicle.

Hannah had only a few more days before she would have to leave my side. The thought frightened both of us, but neither gave wings to the foreboding. The weight of our troubles were heavy on us and that night dinner went uneaten. Before 10pm we both were fast asleep. Me on the couch and Hannah in the recliner adjacent to me.

13

The drive back to Richmond was a long one. Having watched her newly found sister go through such pain reminded her of her own griefs and sorrows from the past. Her husband had not been fond of the idea of her not using her first class ticket to fly home in lieu of rental car and driving the eight hours from Atlanta. She needed the thinking time. A few hours to just process the new trouble that had been giving the direction to her house.

When her phone rang half-way during her travels, it did not surprise her to see it was her mother.

"Hi Mommy."

"Baby Girl, I am been worried sick about you. What's going on? Where are you?"

She wished she could truthfully say nothing, but knew she could not. A part of her secretly prayed that her mother would not say she was having dreams about her or feelings. Those always made her nervous and a case of anxiety was the last thing she needed in the middle of nowhere. Her load was heavy enough.

"I'm fine Mom. You worry too much."

"Yes, and racism in America is a thing of the past."

"Wow, you go straight for the juggler don't you?"

"No, I'm just not a fan of not being told what I already know. So spill."

"Just like that, really Mom? She was stalling for time and they both knew it. The realization was that she wanted to involve her family as less as possible until the killer or killers had been apprehended. Deciding to change the subject she asked about her own birth mother. The one that had adopted her to her best friend and carefully hidden her sordid past only to have it come face to face with it when the adoptive mother died. The same one that was in the last stages of Alzheimer's disease.

"How is Miss. Ann doing?"

On the other line Johanna Hemsley had one or two choices to make. Leave the discussion for when her daughter, the one that God had given her just when she needed a family, was ready to open up or force an unwanted conversation. Her heart told her waiting would be best. She always opened up, eventually.

"Baby I don't think it will be much longer. I believe she is waiting on this mystery person she is always asking to see or talking to."

"Cassie?"

"That would be the one."

"Does she still recognize you mom?"

"Depends on the day."

"Mommy thank you so much for all you are doing to help me. I don't know what I would do without you. Sometimes I feel so torn. Like I abandoned her or something."

"No Hannah Renee Corel-Waiters Chandler Emmanuel you stop that right this instant. You are the best daughter anyone could ever have. You deserve some happiness. And need I remind you that you fly out twice a month and spend the weekend with Ann. Knowing she has no clue who you are most days? If anything ever happened to me dear I would want you and Jesus to be on my team."

Hannah's mind was all over the place now. Her heart in worse conditions. Each time she picked up the pieces to her life disaster, or some tragedy struck. Things beyond her control and there was never anything she could do about it. She missed Jane. Longed to see Michael. Needed to hear the voice of Ian the unlikely minister she loved so much.

"I love you Mom."

"Oh my Lamb, this Cassie thing is just what I felt deep down inside."

"Wow Mom, all that because I said I love you? Really? You are a mess."

"No. I just know my child. Plus, I had a little talk with the Lord."

"Well who can argue with that? Are you going to fill me in on your little prayer meeting?"

"In time."

For the next three hours the mother and daughter converse. It was easy for Hannah to talk to her mother, although it had not always been that way. Life had a way of dealing blows that either forced you to coward and run or fight through the pain. Both had learned to fight for them there was no other recourse. It wasn't until Johanna received an emergency call from a good friend that she said good-bye. This gave Hannah time to prepare for another conversation she had to have before heading home to her husband and children.

She knew exactly where he would be. There was no rational reason why she had waited so long to come. Not wasting any more time she did not bother to even knock on the door. It was late. She was certain no one would be there but him. She was correct.

"Some things never change, do they?"

"Guess not."

He did not look surprised to see her. The sadness in his eyes took her breath away. She did not wait to be asked to take a seat. Trouble threw her into the plush leather high back chair like a victim diving from a sinking ship. She gave him space to say something. Anything. He didn't. She had too.

"T, I can't do this anymore. "He was, is, my second chance T. I have had more sorrow than I have had anything else. He made me happy when I had nothing else. Made me remember what it felt like to smile, love again. Please don't punish me or that. The only reason my life is not perfect now is because my big brother, my hero is not a part of it. I miss you. I need you. We have come too far, been through too much to give up on one another now."

There was no stopping the constant flow of tears that streamed down her face. Months of bottled emotions, raw emotions, hurt, anger, and rejection spilled out and there was nothing either of them could do about it. Gathering herself, she thanked him for the tissue and asked the question that was always with her.

"Why do you hate him so much?"

"Hate who!? I hate no one!" The anger that spewed from him took her back to the first time they met. So much had transpired since the day she waltzed into the office of Dr. Tobias Lincoln Hunt five years or so earlier. She was not moved by him. Time had taught her that his growl was only displaced hurt. Hurt that her decisions had festered. She had no reservations as to his love for her.

"Then why have you not spoken to your best friend in months? Except the pretense you display at work. What happened to our family dinners? The dinners that you always manage to be too busy to attend leaving your wife to constantly make excuses as to your frequent absences."

"I have been busy. You know yourself what it is like to be the wife of a physician. Reverse that and imagine being the physician. One that is in the middle of a life changing research project. Runs a private practice and has a wife and child. Not to mention who is in remission. Or maybe not?"

Jumping to her feet she ran to the big brother who had one foot in this world and the other in the grave when she laid eyes on him for the second time. "What?" She was scared. Terrified and did not attempt to camouflage it. Now in his personal place like the little bit of a bossy sibling she had always been she demanded an answer. "What do you mean?"

Placing his head in his hands he sat at the huge oval desk but still did not answer.

"Talk to me Tobias, please."

The sound of his birth name, in lieu of the pet name she had always used broke something inside of him.

"They found a couple of tumors Hannah."

He looked fatigued. The kind of tired that took life from him. She recognized it. Had worn it. Slept with it and almost lost herself it. Her big brother had given up.

"Well, what did they say about them Tobias?"

"It doesn't look good."

"So, we have been here before remember? You defeated this once and you will do it again."

The silence was too much for her to endure. "Does Kelly know?"

"Not yet. I don't know how to say it. Can't bring myself to say that I have cancer again." Without a second thought she shook him. Hard. "You can't quit T. You will not give up on me. Do you hear me?"

The weight of finding a half-sister she had never known and having to leave her with so much turmoil and despair and on top of that her being pregnant was manifesting itself. Hannah Renee Corel-Waiters Emmanuel is in complete fight mode. To the extent that she did not hear her brother's response.

"Does he treat you well?"

"I don't care what they thing they have found. We will fight this and win Tobias. God answered us before and this time will be no different."

It isn't until he put his hand on her shoulder and repeated his question that she finally heard him.

"Is he good to you? Are you happy Hannah Banana?"

His question had the effect of deflating a balloon. Stunned for a moment about the sudden change of the wind she stared down at him, then eventually returned to her seat. It wasn't that she needed to think about an answer. Gabriel Emmanuel was everything she never knew she needed. She prayed for the words to make her brother understand.

"Every day I wake up with my husband I feel like the luckiest woman on earth. He is patient, kind, and never forces me to do anything. Being me is all I ever have to be with Gabe. He taught me how to love again. He is still teaching me how to love."

"I wondered if I would ever see that sparkle in your eyes again after Brice died. Day and night I worried about you and the children. When I asked you to move out here from San Antonio it was so I could have you close to me. Watch over you. Protect you like I was never afforded the opportunity and make up for so much lost time. For the first time I had my sister. Ally had her aunt and Kelly and I only wanted to nurse you back to life. That day I felt like you had been snatched away from me by a common criminal. All I wanted was a chance to be there for you in the manner in which you always gave of yourself to me and so many others. Gabriel knew this. I felt betrayed."

Trailing off from the conversation like he had something else on his mind Tobias looked out of the window from his third floor office. He wanted to tell his only sister of his trepidations that no woman had ever been able to tame Gabriel Emmanuel, the good looking doctor with a heart of gold. The best friend that he missed immensely. That he worked alongside of each day, spoke to, yet without ever having a real conversation. The one that he would have to trust to care for his sister, his wife and daughter if he did not pull through this sickness.

Hannah looked on. What she saw on his face and oozing from his heart devastated hers. Longing to take the pain of uncertainty away and reassure him she stilled herself from running to him once more. Something in her told her this battle would be between her big brother and God. No one else. She would pray. Be there for him and pray some more but she knew this time the fight with cancer would be a relentless battle for her brother. It took a few seconds to realize that he had begun to speak again. Hannah herself had become lost in thought and unknowingly mirrored the same look she had seen on his face.

"I love you to the moon and back Hannah Banana."

His words made her weep. Her tears caused him to weep. Tobias' attempt to wipe her tears away made her cry even more. They held on to get other tightly for a while. Anyone looking on, not knowing their stories, would have to wonder how the Caucasian doctor with the unruly curls hair and the brown skinned engineer paths had crossed.

Managing to speak through her tears Hannah tells him, "I love you forever times forever T."

"You just had to trump me didn't you?" His playful banter lightened the air a bit.

"Always. Nothing has changed here. I am still the one that is really in charge."

Pretending to groan in exasperation Tobias did not allow her to have the last word. "Only because I let you think you are."

She rolled her eyes and kissed him on the cheek. "Hump! I better get home to my husband before he has the feds looking for me."

"Good idea."

"We will continue this conversation big brother. And...don't dare think you are going to see the oncologist without me."

Convincing her otherwise was a waste of time. Hannah would let nothing stop her and they both were well aware of it. Just before she reached the door he remembered the reason for her trip out of town and called out, "Hey you must catch me up on Cassie." The change in her demeanor made him realize that conversation would need to come sooner than he had planned. Especially when she said, "Too much to tell."

His response, "Never. I will see you next Thursday for my appointment. I will pick you up at 10am."

"Okay, don't be late. You know what that does to my nerves."

Laughing he informed her, "Don't I know it" before the door closed behind her.

14

There were no words when she finally saw her husband after two long weeks. Their eyes met and he forgot to scold her for making him wait the extra hours to see her after suddenly deciding to drive home. It was late and all she wanted was him. All of him. When he reached for her she stepped aside knowing if he started a fire she would have no interest in distinguishing it. There was one more thing to do.

Quietly opening the first door just down the hall her heart melted when she saw her prince. Fast asleep with his stress blankee BJ never stirred when she looked in on him. Not yet two years old he had been every bit of what she had needed in the midst of so much pain when her husband had been tragically killed just before her due date. He was the bittersweet blessing that God sent to help her keep her sanity when life was irrational.

Walking just across the hall she paused before opening the door. Without a doubt little Joy would stir. Even if she was sound asleep, her intuition would alert her that mommy was finally home. How she had missed the smartest preschooler in the world. The strength and inspiration of the family that always reminded them to see the good in everyone and everything. Just as she knew she would, as soon as she cracked the door her little red head lifted from the pillow and her hazel eyes filled with tears. "Mommy...mommy I so missed you mommy." Just hearing her voice made her mother shed a couple of tears. Wiping them quickly she grabbed her daughter, her first miracle that had literally taught her what true love really meant, and held her for a little while.

"Tomorrow we have tea my little Joy, and you can tell me all about what you and daddy and your brother have been doing while I have been away."

"Mommy did you meet her? Did you see Aunt Cassie? Does she have children like you do? Do you look alike? Or does she look like granny Ann?"

Stifling her chortle, Hannah touched the soft red curls that refused to be ruled by anyone, and quietly reminded her, "Tomorrow, over tea." Kissing her on the forehead she left the room and her only daughter was fast asleep before she closed the door.

When she returned to the master bedroom of her home it was dimly lit with candles. The intercom system played soft jazz and in the middle of the room stood the man she had missed so much it caused her physical pain at times. She stopped short upon seeing him. He was breath taking. In every way.

"I've missed you Mrs. Emmanuel." His voice was deep with desire.

Observing the blue eyed, 6'4" dark haired, medium build with the ripping biceps, and strong chin as he offered her a glass of wine and she was too exhausted to scold him. Wine was permitted in his religion. It was not in hers. She took it anyway. She needed him and only him. To make the fantasies she had thwarted about what his luscious lips would do to her a reality. He touched her and she shivered.

She needed to shower but cannot deny him if he touched her. Stepping just out of his reach Hannah hurried into the adjacent bathroom suite with desire as her fuel. Quickly turning on the shower she stripped down to her hazelnut skin. It wasn't long before he hunted her down like prey. His shadow fell over the glass doors of the shower and her heart leaped. She wanted him to join her. He knew.

When he took the luffa from her hand she didn't protest. Becoming lost in his eyes she prayed that little BJ would sleep through the night. Her prayers went unanswered. The loud cries that caused the monitor to static a bit changed the atmosphere like a tone deaf singer. "Hold that thought Mrs. Emmanuel."

"No Gabe, just give me a minute and I will comfort him. You have done a great job the last two weeks and you deserve a break."

"Since when do fathers deserve a break from parenting? Nothing doing, I have our son. You hold on to what I saw in your eyes just a minute ago."

She answered not a word, but the look in her eyes said everything. Kissing her passionately on the lips he grabbed a towel and disappeared. Hannah became lost in thought. Something that had always been dangerous to her. Like a child left alone with a predator she drifted into harms way. Forgetting the massage of the hot water, and the love she knew she had at home, she walked into the unknown. Her mind was not strong enough to withstand the pressure and she plummets into desolation. When her husband returned after several minutes of consoling their toddler his heart stopped when he found her in a fetal position in the corner of the shower. No sound came from her lips, just an inward tormented moan that ravished her body back and forth against the glass wall. To him she was the epitome of strength. She was strong even when she was weak. Nothing stopped her and all knew not to try because when Hannah Emmanuel set her mind to accomplish something she would not be moved.

All he wanted to do was console her. It had taken him a few minutes before he was allowed to even touch her. She was somewhere far away and it took the constant reassuring of his calm voice to lure her out of whatever dark place she had strayed. By the time he dried the long curly brown hair and tucked her into bed she still had not spoken a word. He did not press. She always talked when she was ready, not a moment before. He was just happy she was home. Safe. At least physically anyway. It wasn't until somewhere into the middle of the night that she allowed him into her world. She told her story, but it wasn't with words.

Dr. Gabriel Emmanuel had just fallen asleep when his wife released a small yelp. The restless sleep induced by exhaustion that only worry could deliver by wrestling you down and stripping you of your strength. Each time she moved he stirred. If she breathed different he investigated a possible cause. He desperately worried about his wife. The woman he always dreamt of having. The one he would risk any and everything just to have. The woman he had to have at any cost. The one he could not tame, but enjoyed the thrill of trying. Something was terribly wrong and he knew it. He shuddered to think that her life, their children might be in danger. It was possible. That much he was aware of because he had a secret himself. A little detective secret that had given him reports that made him have nightmares. She must never be privy to this information though.

Pulling her close he whispered, "Talk to me Love. Please." He knew she was wide awake by the way her heart beat. She still did not answer. He attempted to hide his frustration. Sometimes her independence blindsided him and other times it aroused him. This was not one of those times. She was the most stubborn, beautiful, toughest, gentlest, and generous know it all he had ever met, and she owned his heart.

When, after a few minutes, she still did not invite him into her world he knew that the trouble was much bigger than he knew. If only he had Tobias to confer with. The confidant, advisor and friend that he had lost because of an act of betrayal. If only he could do things over. The correct way. Maybe, just maybe he would have been able to steal away and talk to his best friend and brother-in-law. It was somewhere along those thought patterns that it hit him. The heartache he felt, the pain he saw his wife attempt to bear could not be from a sister that she was just getting to know. It was much deeper. He had seen it before. That despair in her eyes. Long ago when he had met her for the first time. Lying on the floor of the hospital elevator.

15

When Dr. Emmanuel entered the office of Dr. Hunt it was a family affair, not a medical emergency. At least that was what he assumed, until he saw his old friend. It wasn't long before his suspicions were confirmed. Not just by the grief that his wife had carried since seeing her when she returned, but the look Tobias bore. One any doctor recognized. One that no medicine could heal. Seeing Tobias' frail body, white face and lifeless eyes took Gabriel Emmanuel's breath away. He held on to the wall, fearing he would not make it to the high back chair in his office. Neither physician spoke, but they both quickly came to an understanding.

More ten minutes passed before either man spoke. After an eternity it was Tobias who finally scattered the iron gate. "Do you love her?" The answer came without hesitation. "With all my heart." Eye to eye the two searched for truths and only found regret. Gabe was lost in the time that had been wasted. The senseless battles he had fought. The pride he refused to release. Tobias was just tired. He only wanted to set his house in order and find the peace that had escaped him all for the past few months.

"Take care of her." Those words allowed the cement that had held Gabe's feet to disintegrate. In two giant steps he crossed the room and threw his arms around the slumped figure sitting at the desk. No other words came. Just tears. Bitter, resentful, salty tears that stained the medical reports on Tobias' desk.

The next two hours were spent not burying the hatchet, that had been done the minute Gabe had crossed the room and embraced his best friend and brother. They were spent taking care of family matters. The discussions that only God could help you adhere. What I want. What you should do. How it should be carried out. Where. What. If. All caused Gabe to quiver at the knees, constantly losing at the battle of keeping his right foot from shaking. A clear sign he was in despair. He did not conceal it. Tobias never said a word. Not about his knowing that is friend, colleague, brother and confidant did not know how to handle the finalities of his life. He was still coming to terms with it himself.

After leaving the medical offices Gabe took his lunch. Having no intentions to eat, he was oblivious to when he could eat again, he sat at the park down the street. Back into the parking space he sat with the window down. He looked at the stack of legal documents that sat next to him and broke. He wished he knew God like his wife did. He longed to find solace in her, but the stark realization that this would break her made him feel further distressed.

He watched a family play with their two small children. They reminded him of his own. The little boy, no more than two or three constantly giggled as his father pushed him in the swing. His mother was busy playing with his older sister. They took turns coming down the slide. They appear to be happy. He wondered what their story was and if the picture perfect images were their true reality. He had waited so long to find true happiness. A lifetime. Before the conversation the only missing piece from his life was

Tobias. Now he was devastated upon learning that he would be leaving all of them forever. Something in him worried tremendously that his wife would not be able to handle another loss. Not this one. Not the brother she had searched for and found. The only family she was ever privy to or had a real relationship with. She had already buried a mother, a husband, a child and now this. His head hurt and he felt sick. It wasn't until he had to open the door of the car and part ways with the big breakfast he had eaten did he understand just how broken he was.

"Sir...sir...are you well? I don't mean to intrude or anything."

Embarrassed, he looked up to see the woman that had been having family time in the park serval feet away. She reminded him of someone, he just did not know who at the moment.

"I'm fine thank you Ms."

"I have a ginger ale in my car. It could help to settle your stomach a bit."

He noticed the husband in the background whisper her name in an attempt to get her moving in the right direction. She was non-compliant. Before an answer could be spoken she was at her vehicle retrieving the can of pop as promised.

"Sorry it's a little warm, but that should work to your advantage."

Looking up at not two, but four pairs of eyes Gabe took the drink. "Thank you very much. You are most kind."

He saw the sigh of relief from the husband in waiting. Feeling he should do something more, he waved at the gentleman and said, "Thanks again" and attempted to close the door. He wondered why neither of them were bothered by the small puddle of waste outside of his car. He concluded that it must be the parenting small children had prepared them for such things. It was not until the short dark skinned lady with unusually long hair spoke again that he realized his conclusion may have been wrong.

"You are most welcomed Dr. Emmanuel."

It was evident his look of curiosity was not masked when the stranger reacted to it. "I see you from time to time at the hospital." She extended her hand, "Carolyn Hester, pleased to make your acquaintance."

"You mean the Carolyn Hester, surgeon and mastermind?"

"Well...if you say so." They both laughed.

She was stunning. He was amused and amazed at what scrubs could conceal. Not to mention a bit curious about the husband that was so comfortable being in the background. When the smaller of the two children began to cry she immediately said, "Well, duty calls. See you around and I hope you feel better." With that they left Gabe with his ginger ale and his grief.

Grief that he had only had twice in his life. Twice that had been enough to turn his life completely upside down. Grief that had always driven him to sex with other woman or a bottle. But that was a past life that his wife did not know anything about. One he had utterly abandoned with one touch from Hannah. The past was where he planned to keep the awful pain he had caused others because of his weaknesses. Until that morning his life had been perfect. Now what he thought was dead had come rushing back. The urges, the desires, the pain, the uncertainty.

It wasn't the sick feeling in his stomach that terrified him. It was the rushing burn of erotic desire he felt when he had looked at Carolyn Hester. For a split second he imagined having her thrown against a hospital wall hearing her scream for him to give her more. He was sweating. Those thoughts could cost him everything. He loved his wife and she had been the only woman to tame him, until now. Hannah needed him. He needed her. He had his family. His career. Why did he want to have sex with a stranger?

It did not take long for him to locate the pager of Dr. Hester. When the voice on the other line spoke, "This is Dr. Hester. What may I do for you?" they both knew the answer to the question. Each knew it would not be long before the inevitable would become their reality.

16

I spent most of my waking hours at Major's side. It was much easier now that I had police protection. The staff were understanding and patient with me, with us. That eased a little of my stress. Normally I hated pity, but the bigger my belly grew and the longer I resided at the apartment I began to change my view. My days normally consisted of eating hot cereal for breakfast and a piece of fruit. Then making a sandwich for lunch, I exited for the hospital somewhere between nine in the morning and noon. It just depended on what the police protection suggested. It was one less thing to worry about.

Not quite understanding why, this particular morning I was having such a hard time. Emotionally, I was already spent and it was only mid-morning. Life weighed heavy on me. My days ran together and I never really paid attention to dates. The only day I really looked forward to was hearing that the killer of my parents had been found. So when the news reporter gave the time and the date it should not have been a big deal, but it was. It broke me. That is when she realized it would have been her mother's sixty-fourth birthday. The tears would not stop. Trying to hide my pain I retreated back to my room. My thoughts would not shut off. My need to honor my parents in some way was ever present. For the purpose of my safety having a memorial service could not be a consideration. That reality check made my mood even darker.

Resting on my bed, my thoughts drifted to Hannah. I missed her immensely and wondered what she was doing. Being around her made me feel better, stronger. Kind of like the old me before I relinquished who I was for a bad relationship. I found it necessary to restrict my calling so I wouldn't intrude in her life. There was no way for me to confirm my thoughts, but I felt as though my newly found sister was having troubles of her own. It was hard to camouflage trouble. I could heard it in her voice each time we spoke, but I did not pry. My life alone was enough to cause anyone to run, but she stayed anyway. There was just so much to deal with, and then there was the little matter of becoming a mother.

Besides my safety, knowing that it wouldn't be long before my baby would be born was my greatest concern. That frightened me more than anything. I did not want to be alone. The classes were helping me understand the process, but how could I possibly be ready for an infant with my life still in shambles? With the killer still on the loose and no suspect? I owned two homes and could not set foot in either of them. My career was non-existent. I worried about finances. How long could I survive with what we had saved up? The medical bills, the house payments and everything required for the baby was just too much. Major was progressing, but his recovery could take months, possibly years. With setbacks of infections, rehabilitation mishaps and lack of staff all being contributors, I did not know when normal would ever be a part of my life again.

Then there was the fact that I was not who I thought I was in the first place. Adopted. What do you do when you find out you have a mother other than the one that raised you? How do you begin to handle knowing that when you finally meet her you still won't ever get to introduce yourself? She was dying. One day, Angela, gave birth to me. Yet, another family raised me and never thought I deserved to know about it. Nothing in my life made sense. I'd made up my mind, even if she could not recognize me I had to meet her. Somehow I believed that her heart would know. Just like Hannah's and my heart had connected I was sure she would know.

Besides trouble, the only regular thing in my life was a neighbor that would not stop pestering me. It was all in the name of concern of course. Life being what it was, as soon as I found a comfortable position in my bed, the doorbell rang. There was no guessing as to who it would be. Groaning within me and my frustration slipped to my feet. I was already regretting my decision to go to the hospital in the afternoon instead of morning. There was no point in trying to ignore the constant knocking. She knew I was at home and she would not disappear like I secretly wished she would. I did not have to alert my protection, they were already in position just in case.

Tale Carmen was as ordinary as ordinary could possibly be, until he smiled, and then the world stopped. The southern California native only wanted to be a police officer since the age of three. Twenty-six, sandy hair and cartoon like voice, he was way too serious about being undercover. Each time the doorbell rang, knowing exactly who was behind it, he gave me the look. After that, he placed his hand on his hoister and positioned himself in the kitchen. Reading a book, having a snack or just surfing the net, but always ready to take action. When he was on duty, me and my unborn child were a thousand percent his priority. His alleged wife, Cynthia Faison was always at her place of employment because she worked the day shift and he worked the night shift at the same nuclear plant.

The moment I opened the door to my neighbor, regret and I followed her back to the couch. I was annoyed when I thought I saw a smirk on Officer Tale's face. It did not take long before the conversation was all about her new boyfriend. I made a sincere attempt not to be the eye rolling kind, but I was failing miserably. Uncertain if it had to do with me becoming more uncomfortable in my pregnancy, I was very high on the irritability charts.

Marlene, or queenmarlene according to her Snapchat, was enough all by herself. She worked, but did not have to because she had money. At least that's what she told me. Pushing somewhere around the forty club she was as free spirited as I have ever seen. No children. No husband. New Yorker from head to toe, by way of the south mind you. She was a burglar's worse nightmare. If she wasn't on her part time job she was either at mass or meditating. Even during conversations with me she would without warning take a yoga position. It was nothing out of the ordinary for her to check in with her inner self. "The atmosphere is cluttered. I think you have bad energy in here. The sky looks funny." Anything was a reason to cause her to close her eyes in mid conversation, hands extended, legs crossed and make strange noises.

This particular day she was thrilled because he was taking her to the new restaurant she longed to have dinner. On and on she went about how he was the one she had waited for and she was sure the great one sent him.

"Oh you just have to meet him. He is stopping by later and I will bring him right over."

Her voice escalated a few octaves when she was excited and like she was totally excited. Not wanting to be rude I did my best to tell her in no uncertain terms that I already had plans that afternoon.

"Marlene I'm going to have to take a raincheck."

Looking offended she got a little too close for comfort and pried. "Well what ever could you be doing?"

Forgetting to use her accent she resorted to the southerner she really was. I almost laughed. Apparently my undercover officer did because he texted me an emoji that is laughing so hard it is crying. Ready for her to make her exit I forgot about etiquette and stood up and told her just why.

"I have an appointment Marlene. As a matter of fact I really should be getting ready to leave now."

Making a slow recovery she reluctantly stood and said, "Another time I suppose." Slowly walking to the door she gave a little wave but did not leave until she promised to, "Make good on my raincheck." I kicked myself several times.

The truth is I had already seen her boyfriend. He was creepy. There wasn't a time I looked out the window that he wasn't standing somewhere near my yard. He always saw me before I saw him. Never making eye contact he would not say one word. Nothing. Something inside me knew Marlene's new friend had something to hide, but that was none of my business. He was probably married or something. Or maybe he was only using her, whatever the case I had no intentions of ever meeting him.

17

It was a Wednesday morning and storming outside. The kind of storm that uprooted trees, sent trash receptacles and shopping carts on long journeys and made children cry. I was exhausted and I felt like the walls were caving in on me. Major was better in many ways but not enough to come home. His doctors wanted to move him to a home where he could continue to be rehabilitated. Although excited I was sure he would not be there when our child was born. The only person I had in the world was Hannah. That is when I decided that we must have a talk. Not thinking about the hour I called her with only one thing on my mind.

"Hello...Taylor..., is everything okay?" The surprise call at such an odd hour had rattled Hannah.

"Hi Hannah. Yes everything is fine. I mean still the same, but no worse." I was rambling and did not know why. I mean all I wanted to do was ask a total stranger to do the impossible.

"Okay, you're lying, but you already know this."

Her frankness was something I was still getting used to. Hannah said what was on her mind and that was that.

"Well, I was just wondering if you meant what you said. You know, about me moving there with you."

"Taylor, I don't say things I don't mean."

There was silence on the phone. I really did not know how to come out and say it, but knew I must.

"I would like to take you up on the offer. If it still stands of course."

Her response is something I will always remember.

"Finally. I have prayed for this since the day I first met you Taylor."

She did not see my tears, but they rushed down my face. Tears of relief. She would be there for me. If I had learned nothing else from Hannah Renee, it was she kept her word. I was moving to Richmond, Virginia. I did not know how, but I was certain it would happen.

18

Standing in the shadows Gabe watched as the small processional arrives. First the police escort, then the ambulance, a car he did not recognize and then another police officer.

Finally he could put more than just a face to the people that had interrupted his life completely. Looking a bit anxiously he scanned the cars for the only concern he had in the world. At last he saw her, but she does not notice him. His heart skips a beat. He releases a breath he was unaware he had been holding.

It took only seconds for him to close the gap between him and his wife. She was his everything. When he kissed her it was more than an I missed you and I am glad you are home. Safe. It was the secrets within. The ones that he had no idea how she would handle once she knew the truth. Pushing those thoughts to the side he bruised himself being useful. There was much to do in so little time. He wanted to get Major settled into the rehabilitation home, me and my undercover police officers settled into their home so he could have his wife back.

By the end of the day none thought it could have possibly gone in the direction that it took. What should have taken only a couple of hours took eight. From missing paperwork, to misunderstandings and heated discussions, by the time Hannah pulled into her driveway she was completely drained. For the next few weeks this became her story. Their story.

Gabe worked more and more. Taylor's belly grew bigger and Miss Ann grew sicker. No news about the opened murder cases. No word on how long all of our lives would be turned upside down. Some days all of our thoughts got the better of us. Tempers flared, misunderstandings, medical emergencies came and the only thing that made it worth it was we called each other family.

Life became one big blur. A blur that encompassed life and death. Pain and joy. Four others and I fly to Texas and met Miss Ann. Less than forty-eight hours later she died in her sleep. Major learned to walk again. Small steps, but they were still steps. Tobias grew worse. Hannah had suspicions. It was a cycle. One all of us wished would end soon. This cycle lead right up to the day I went to my doctor's appointment and learned I was in active labor.

It all went very fast. By the time Hannah arrived at the hospital I was ready to push. Major watched on video call as I gave him what he always dreamt of having, a child. When the doctor announced, "It's a girl" for the first time in months we had something to be happy about. We all had a reason to hope again. The tiny little five pound baby girl, with the coal black hair, and quiet cry was the rainbow in the middle of the storm.

What they do not know is that I had a plan. One that included going back to Atlanta as soon as my little miracle was old enough. My life was going to fall into place, I was going to force it herself. Seeing my daughter for the first time had given me the strength I needed to fight for a normal life. That was exactly what I was going to do.

It only took eight weeks. From the moment I heard my physician give me the all clear, I knew what I must do. It had been the only real plan I could come up with for a long time. The only answers to putting my life back together I knew were in Atlanta. Something or someone was there to free me from the prison my life had before. I was grateful Major was becoming stronger and stronger. Joyful about the new addition to our family. My sister Hannah was nothing short of a rock for me. Even though she had suffered loss after loss, she still managed to be there for me. Still, it was time for me to take charge of my own life. Fear was suffocating me and I must face it head on.

19

When the three cars pull into the driveway of the suburban Atlanta home none of the passengers moved. All waited for the command from me, Mrs. Taylor Jasper. I contemplated pulling into the garage, but talked myself out of it. The enemy, whomever they were needed to know I was back and ready to fight. Thinking about my precious little Hope back at the hotel gave me strength. The fact that I had been unable to breastfeed did not make leaving my baby any easier. Hope Renee Jasper was the light I had to see to keep pressing forward.

It was surprisingly quiet for a Saturday morning. Usually the sound of weed eaters and lawn mowers serenaded the flowers and the trees, but not this day. I was interested at how many for sales signs I had seen on the way in, but said nothing. Who would care? It was a past life I planned to divorce as soon as I found the answers I needed to start over again.

After about ten minutes of sitting we entered the house. Not because I was ready, but because my little hyperactive, attention deficit disorder Robocop was antsy. Complying with orders, I allowed the gentlemen to enter first and waited for the all clear. Of the six of us, two would secure the area, then return for my sister and I, while a couple of friends from the local police department monitor the front and back areas of the house.

My inner peace was immediately depleted the moment I stepped into the living room. The last few months of my life came crashing down on my already crippled soul. The trip home from having been unfaithful to my abusive husband. The smell of his decomposed body lingering in the air. The voice that ordered me not to move, the gun shots, the footsteps, the cold…

"Taylor…Taylor, are you well?" Hannah's voice did just what it was intended to do. Bring me back to reality. To everyone else I appeared fine, but not to my sister. In just a few short months Hannah knew me as if we had grown up together. I only shook my head yes. I knew my voice would betray me.

It wasn't long before we slowly walked through several rooms. I was feeling fatigued from the trip and the post pardon I battled and fought back tears. I turned the hall corner with the intent to go down to one of the bedrooms Finn nor I frequented. Maybe it was reentering the home that had cause me so much pain. The abuse. The murder of my first husband. The attempted murder of me and my baby and so much more, too much more and I am sure it contributed to the way I was feeling.

It was my first time being back in the house since that morning when the hand with the leather glove had covered my mouth. I regretted coming. It was too soon. In an attempt to hurriedly exit the house where I had found my late husband shot in the head I stumbled. Trying to grab the wall for balance I hit it; hard. Believing the sudden clicking sound I heard on impact was my worn body, I stood in shock when a door slowly swung open. I screamed!

Officer Bain Green was the first to arrive, gun drawn, calling for back up in the process. Fresh out of high school he was undercover as a distant cousin of mine. The only officer willing to work the weekend so that I could tie up some loose ends. Detective Whit followed close behind and Hannah along with him. Kicking the door with such force that the top hinge fell off Bain put his gun into the dark room. Right on cue both he and detective Whitt produced a flashlight simultaneously. Back to back they scanned the room while turning in a small circle. It was only when Hannah waltzed into the room and hit the light switch was there finally a "Clear!" By this time Atlanta's finest was everywhere. No one was in anyway prepared for what they saw, especially me.

"Breathe Taylor" Hannah demanded, "Breathe!" Her voice was not gentle. She allowed no room for argument. The rapidness of my pulse, my pale and clammy skin and the look of terror in my eyes assured Hannah that I was having a panic attack.

"Do we need to call an ambulance Mrs. Emmanuel?" Officer Green sounded a little concerned. He had gained a particular fondness of Taylor having been her personal body guard for so long. Hannah waved her hand in dismissal and continued to give orders to me.

Within a few seconds I was sitting on the floor in the hall. I had checked out. It was my way of coping. Hannah left my side for no more than a minute and returned with a big mauve bag. Reaching inside she grabbed a bottle of pills and gave one to me. Without question I took the medication and swallowed it without the assistance of a beverage. I moved back against the wall, put my head back and closed my eyes. Hannah stayed right beside me.

When I recovered I had to see the reason the police officers whispered and Hannah pondered. With Hannah directly behind me I stopped short at what I saw. My thoughts did not have time to wonder before an officer told me, "Do not touch anything." My brain and my eyes were in total disagreement. Unbelief and shock being the reason for the feud. I forgot to ask how a secret room could be in the home that I built; that I had the blue prints to. That was minor reasoning compared to the merchandise inside.

At first glance the secret room mimicked a theater room, but instead of chairs, cameras filled the front half of it. Shelves line the walls and on them sat rows of small tapes. Mounted on the wall was a small flat screen television. Next to it was a cot, a pillow and blanket. The back half of the room was different. Used for storage of items I had never seen. Paintings, silver, figurines and not a few small pieces of jewelry. Rings, necklaces, earrings, cuff links and hairpins. I could not understand what I was seeing or why. My only rational thought was that I must have been in the wrong residence. But she remembered disarming the alarm, turning the key and walking in the place she had at one time called home. She had seen the bullet holes from the shootout. The toppled furniture from exiting in a hurry. All of it reminded her that she was indeed in the right house, but the secret room remained a mystery.

Within just a few minutes all I figured out that my late husband had been spying on me since day one. Trying to process the information I wanted to kill him all over again in her head. The thought never crossed my mind that the cameras would not only have recorded my coming and going, but perhaps the killer's as well.

Having my mind wonder back to the painful memories I had lived in what should have been my dream home was heart wrenching. Seeing them play out before my eyes was something altogether different. Every time I saw myself take a blow from Finn it was like having a knife to my heart. Then the shame encompassed me. Not only was I watching the videos, but a room full of strangers were also watching. Not only were her intimate moments with Finn on display, but the cruel ones as well. Each time he touched me in pain or passion.

Going in the team developed a system to allow only myself to review the sensitive matters. Having someone watch me making love to her husband was beyond uncomfortable. For me those moments were real, but for Finn it had all been a game. I saw the difference when his mistress was seen pleasuring him video after video. Although I knew I should have fast forwarded, I just sat there. Then Hannah stepped in and did what I could not do. My heart did not want to watch, but my mind did not respond to the messages being sent. Seeing another woman in my home, in my bed, with my husband was shocking. Even though I had moved on to another life the old one still plagued me.

The tapes were not labeled and in no particular order. The only plan the group had was to watch them in sections starting with the top shelf. It was grueling but no one wanted to stop. We all felt we were close to a major breakthrough.

Somewhere around eleven that night, when all were exhausted and nerves were on edge something happened.

"Wait! Rewind, go back please." Officer Carmen and Detective Whitt gave one of his looks. When the video went back to the part in question I blurted out, "I know that man. I've seen him before."

"I need you to really really think. Just take your time and allow it to come to you Mrs. Jasper." There was a gleam in Officer Green's eyes.

"The hair and the face are fuzzy, but the eyes I remember. Mysterious, cold, yet familiar."

"Can you place him in Georgia or in Virginia?" Detective Whitt interjected.

"Not sure just yet, but I have seen him I am certain."

The fog of disappointment was suffocating. Deciding whether to call it a night or morning, depending on how you viewed it, we prepared to shut things down. Until Detective Whitt, who was still watching the video and I yelled at the same moment. Her "I remember!" and his "Oh my God!" turned heads and fate. Detective Whitt demanded attention with his announcement of "We have found our killer ladies and gentlemen."

I was sobbing at that point. A sorrowful, sad groaning that was barely audible. The tears that had already stained my silk blouse were memoirs of my deep disturbance.

"Talk to me Taylor, please." Hannah's calm voice only made it worse.

What I did not know was that the man I could now identify isn't the killer seen in the video. The person seen leaving the former home of Finn and Taylor Bardo at the time of his murder was none other than his mistress. The beautiful, blond haired, blue eyed Marlo Santeen Miller was seen quickly leaving our home at the estimated the time of death. Just before she opened the front door she placed a twenty-two caliber in her designer purse.

What I knew was that the person in question, the one I recognized, lived right next door to me posing as the boyfriend of my neighbor Marlene. The same person I saw several times a week before moving to Virginia to have my baby. The very one that always waved, but never said one word to me. The most charming middle aged, by appearance anyway, thoughtful, according to Marlene, handsome but strangest person I had ever encountered.

Why would he be my house? Certain it was no coincidence it chilled me to my bones. Now, that instinct I was known for in her field had returned.

There was always something familiar about him I could not put her finger on. His presence almost spooked her. No matter where Marlene and I conversed, he was never far away. Always within a listening distance.

Remembering the conversations with Marlene about her beau that seems to just fall from heaven made me want to just kick herself. "Denise (my alias name) he is just perfect.

I was carrying my groceries to my car one day and he just appeared out of nowhere to give me a helping hand. Such a gentlemen. He is always available no matter what time or day I call him. He truly is the man I have waited for so long to come into my life. He is just perfect" On and on she went until I always made up some excuse to end the conversation.

All I knew was that there were six bedrooms in my house and no one was leaving until I had more answers. No one, not even Detective Howard Whitt, despite the nonstop calls his wife made. I now knew that I finally had an answer to the mystery to the death of my first husband, but the search for my parents' killer had only just begun. I was sure the mystery man in the video had everything to do with it.

www.ingramcontent.com/pod-product-compliance
Lightning Source LLC
Chambersburg PA
CBHW051924220626

47052CB00003B/571